Prologue

A gunshot combined with screams could be heard coming from the living room of the 18th century stately manor. The manor already suspected of being haunted created an eerie atmosphere and now with the screams ringing out created a horrifying experience to the now awakened ten-year-old peering through the small gap of the stairway of the second floor overlooking the living room.

"Take whatever you want, just leave us alone," quivered the homeowner.

Wrestling the gun off the masked assailant, the homeowner was pushed to the ground and held at gunpoint once again. Shaking his head, the homeowner this time took him seriously.

The assailant's accomplice headed towards the stairway.

"I will go and get the rest of the cash boss," he shouted. Heading towards the ten-year-old who was still peering through the gap, they jumped up and snuck to the room opposite, hiding in the closet.

"Where the fuck is it," mumblings in the adjacent bedroom. "Ha! Come to daddy." With a sense of triumph, the accomplice marched back down the stairs. The ten year old snuck back out to their starting point at the top of the stairway.

"You have everything you want now get the hell out of my house," the homeowner

shouted.

"I am afraid we can't do that. You and your wife have seen too much." The assailant, grabbing the gagged woman by the throat.

"We can't take our chances."

Two simultaneous gunshots could be heard. The ten year old gasped in shock and to avoid detection ran back to the room opposite. From this point this well privileged kid knew his life would change forever.

The police were trying their best to console the ten year old, but they were so shaken by the night's events there was total silence. Lying in front of their face were two dead bodies, in a puddle of blood. The hero of this heartbroken kid gone just like that, over a bit of cash and jewellery.

The police took the kid away from the crime scene and one final look behind them, their eyes welled up partly sadness but mainly anger.

Chapter 1
Somewhere in the Caribbean,
38 years later

"The first helicopters should be landing tomorrow, sir," the young assistant mentioned.

"Is everything else setup, in accordance with the plan?" said the tall, suited individual. Dan the young assistant, explained that it was all setup, but he still had something on his mind.

"Mr Newman, it is all setup but are you sure you are doing the right thing." Cowardly, questioning the orders of his boss.

"Dan don't ever question my judgement or else it will be the last thing you do. Make yourself useful and make me a drink." Annoyed at the questioning, Walter Newman, chucked his previous drink towards the office door just missing the head of Dan. Walter spun around and continued to stare at the newspaper cut outs on his office wall, something that he has been doing every day for nearly 20 years.

Walter Newman was a powerful billionaire, mostly inherited his money from his father.

His father being a property magnate who had connections to politicians, is how this tropical island as well as all the other property around the world came into the hands of Walter.

Walter visualised this island as his workplace, sanctuary, and headquarters of his worldwide empire with his one and only confidant, Dan. Dan was not just his right-hand man but his only person he would speak to daily.

Ten years ago, Dan was down on his luck just went through a divorce, no kids. Walter gave him a new lease of life. He may not agree with a lot of Walter's actions but who is he to argue against, he feels indebted to his boss. His latest plan he didn't know the full ins and outs, but Walter had been planning it for years. Ever since one traumatic event as a child, Walter has had that vengeful look in his eye wanting to make right from wrong.

Not many people came to the island, mainly only business associates, politicians, or the odd crime lord. However, they were only ever allowed to stay at the Northern part of the island, where the guest living quarters were, sublime beaches and butlers to cater for their every need. They were never allowed to go to the southern part of the island where Walter's beach house was and another building which has been in construction for many years.

Walter has always told guests it is a hotel that is in construction, why would they question a successful property billionaire on his latest venture. This is the life of Walter Newman, rarely leaving his 80-acre Caribbean paradise.

Walter standing all alone in his office staring at the newspaper cut outs was a daily thing for him. Always been alone, never married or had any kids. He has felt that he could not trust anyone enough to form a life partnership with. He felt they would steal his money. Walter would tend to get his thrills by flying in prostitutes from around the world to his island. Just like everyone else, they would stay at the Northern part of the island. Once the deed had been done, they were paid and flown back to where they came from. Making them feel worthless.

Dan brought his boss the drink he ordered. "Have we got the five that we require, Dan?" said Walter.

"Like I mentioned before, the helicopters are coming from tomorrow."

"Are all the rooms ready, everything needs to go to plan" Dan getting very frustrated showed him a blueprint of the adjacent building under construction. Not fully aware of his true intentions.

"I really think you should sleep on it. It is a really big plan you have sir."

"Dan, I do not like my ideas being criticised. I am making right from the wrongs. Something my father would be proud of."

"I understand that but what if something goes wrong," Dan mumbled.

"When have I ever failed in life Dan. Look where you are now. A beautiful tropical island in the Caribbean," boasted Walter.

"I am pretty annoyed with you today, Dan. Get yourself off and I will see you bright and early tomorrow."

"Get the hell out of my office," yelled Walter.

With a big smirk on his face, he went over to his desk and pulled out a bottle of Scotch and a cigar. The bottle had never been opened. Walter had been told to only open once he has accomplished what he wants in life. The time was now.

Dan having arrived back at his villa complex on the island. Was for the first time in his life debating his loyalty to Walter. This is the same guy who lifted him up when he was at his lowest. Dan will always be grateful to him. However, looking up he could see evil.

Standing on his balcony, Walter with a glass of scotch and cigar. He was finally satisfied enough that he was about to accomplish his goal. Justice will be served.

Chapter 2

Having lost both parents at ten years old, birthdays were shitty for this now 18 year old. Foster parents tried their best for the previous seven birthdays to make them memorable, but they were never the same since that horrible night that still lives in the memory of this now young adult venturing out on their own.

It took six months after that night, for the arrest to happen and even longer for the judge to make a choice, the wrong choice they believed. At least 30 years in prison for robbery and murder. They wanted the death penalty, they felt assailant had not got their comeuppance.

"The good news, now you have turned 18, it is all yours," said the lawyer. The 18 year old now looking jubilant, now as a purpose in the world. This meant the 18th century eerie manor the setting of the worst moment in their life was now in their possession.

"I think it is time now to re visit the family home," the 18 year old mentioned.

"Are you ready?" the lawyer questioned.

"I want to bring back the good memories I had in there." The 18 year old staring at the lawyer.

The lawyer handed them a piece of paper with list of names on them. "These are all the addresses of the property your father had."

"Also, a couple of companies your father had an interest in, the stakes in these are worth big money," highlighted the lawyer. "Something to consider for the future," whispered the lawyer.

"What about the cash?"

"The police couldn't retrieve any of the cash stolen in the house from that night," stressed the lawyer. "However, your mother and father left you money in a trust fund and now you have turned 18 you can access part of it."

"How much are we talking?" The 18-year-old questioned.

"At last count including the interest accumulated, just over nine million dollars."

"When you turn 21 you will get another nine million dollars."

The 18 year old knew his parents had money but not the amount they had just been told. Also, this is not considering the list of properties on the piece of paper handed to them by the lawyer. Looking gobsmacked, they walked out of the room to get some fresh air and take it all in.

"I just need a few signatures, then we are all done, "said the lawyer.

"After that we are going to my family home." The 18 year old ordered the lawyer.

Chapter 3

"The first helicopter has arrived sir," said Dan. Walter stood up and headed towards Dan.

"Excellent if you welcome them and take them to their room. I will pop over and introduce myself later," demanded Walter.

"I will do sir," replied Dan.

"Remember Dan, let them enjoy themselves for the first few days and then the games will begin." Walter with a big smile on his face.

"Welcome to Newman Cay. I am Dan the island caretaker also personal assistant to the owner. You must be Jason, our first guest today."

"Thank you for inviting me. When I got the invite, I thought it was a joke. It is amazing what you are doing for me." Jason said excitedly whilst shaking Dan's hand.

Jason was in his early 50's, scruffy looking with a beard. He was older than both Dan and Walter. He had an unusual scar on his lower arm.

"That looks like a painful scar you have there," said Dan.

"It was painful, an incident with fire many years ago," explained Jason, rolling the sleeves back down on his shirt.

"Follow me this way please." Dan ushering Jason along. Whilst walking together Dan was showing Jason the sites of the island until they arrived at a room.

"Here we are, this is your room. Direct access to the beach." Dan mentioned to Jason. Giving Jason a piece of paper. "Before I forget, this is the itinerary for the week." Dan pointing to the piece of paper.

"The third day there is an important meal in the main complex at the southern part of the island. This being the only time you can go to that part of the island. Guests are restricted to the northern part." Dan was clearly explaining to Jason.

"However, I feel this is the nicer part of the island anyway." They both laughed.

"What happens if I fancy something to eat," asked Jason.

"As explained in the itinerary, use the phone in the room and call that number and your own personal butler will get you whatever you want, anytime of the day."

"Is there anything I can get you now, like a cocktail" asked Dan.

"I no longer drink alcohol. I will have a non-alcoholic cocktail, what they called Mocktails or something," laughed Jason.

Dan rushed out of the room and headed back to the side of the island. Another helicopter could be seen landing on the helipad in the distance.

In the office in the main beach house, Walter was staring once again at the newspaper cut outs on the wall. The smile ever growing on his face. Pulling the bottle of scotch out of his drawer and lighting a cigar.

Helicopter landed just outside from the beach house and another individual disembarked. Dan ran towards to introduce himself.

"Good morning, you must be Jack. I am Dan the island caretaker. If you would like to follow me, I will show you to your room."

Even though they were on a tropical island surrounded by the most beautiful sea in the world, Jack oddly requested for a room away from the sea, like he had a fear of water.

"I have had a tough time in my life, and this seems the perfect program for me, thank you," said Jack.

Dan walked alongside Jack providing him with the same itinerary as Jason and explaining the rules of the island. Dan had a sense of regret when providing a personal tour for the two guests so far. Knowing that it is not all it seems.

Walter finally came out of his beach house and took a quick ride on a golf buggy to the northern part of the island, making his way down to the guest rooms. Once he got there Dan had just finished up with the latest guest.

"Hello, I am Walter the owner of the island, boastfully telling Jason.

"Thanks very much for having us. I look forward to taking part in the program," Jason said excitedly,

"As mentioned by Dan there is an important meal which is an opportunity for all the guests to meet each other over a nice food and drink," said Walter

"I look forward to it," replied Jason. Walter then headed round the corner to introduce himself to Jack and advise him of the same information.

By the time Walter had finished introducing himself to the two guests, a few more helicopters arrived. Dan, being on the ball was already helping the guests disembark from the helicopters. Just like the previous two guests, Dan was introducing himself and heading towards the villas on the Northern part of the island, which housed the guest rooms.

"I am Walter Newman, owner of the island. I am glad you have made it safely," with a smirk on his face.

"Thank you for giving me this opportunity. I am truly grateful," said Cameron. He was one of the new guests to arrive. Cameron was a young-looking lad with a very noticeable face tattoo.

"You two must be Damian and Eli. I welcome you both," said Walter.

Walter seemed to have a keen interest in Eli to the point it was kind of creepy. Eli never batted an eyelid as he was being treated like royalty for the first time in his life.

Dan was giving the last guests their itinerary and like the previous two guests explained the important meal on the third day. The guests with delight on their faces settled into their guest rooms on his paradise island, something they were not used to.

Dan headed back to Walter's office looking quite annoyed but glad this part was all over.

"Dan, here is a Scotch. Thank you for your work today. So happy you have remained on side. It must be hard, but you will definitely be rewarded," stated Walter looking back at the wall with the newspaper cut outs.

Begrudgingly, Dan took a sip and whispered, "anything for you sir."

Chapter 4

"This must be a real shock for you," sympathised the police officer. Mr Jackson, whose life changed only last year, when he became a millionaire on his 18th birthday, following the traumatic death of his parents 8 years prior to this. Now another year older his life was back down to the same level of pain he had back then. Hearing the news that both his foster parents as well has his two foster siblings had been killed in an arson attack.

Mr Jackson had some level of loyalty to his foster parents who had raised him since he was ten. He even took their surname, Jackson. He gave them one of the many houses he had inherited from his father to his foster family. Now it was burnt to a crisp like building in a war-torn country.

"Is there anything we can do for you, Mr Jackson," exclaimed the officer.

"Ensure whoever is responsible for this gets what they deserve," Mr Jackson said angrily.

"Don't worry we will ensure, they get the fitting punishment," the officer said.

The police at this point had no idea who was responsible or motive they had.

Initially Mr Jackson thought it could be one of his many business associates out for revenge. Mr Jackson got his straight to the point business acumen from is biological father. However, even he does not think anyone would sink that low and burn a family home down.

Has he looked back with anger in his eyes it brought back the same memories of his childhood with that same vengeful look, once again walking from a crime scene.

A dimming light with the tapping of feet in the eerie corridor of the courthouse. It had been several months of investigation. Mr Jackson had money to burn on private investigators to hunt down the murderers of his foster family, with the police efforts now exhausted. Finally, it was the justice that should be served. The courthouse should be the place where prisoners see the last bit of the outside world before rotting away in a prison cell. For some reason he knew it was not to be.

"25 years," as the gavel slammed on the desk. "Order" shouted the judge to the disgusted courtroom.

"Death Penalty," screamed the friends and family of the victims. Mr Jackson looked with anger towards the prisoner, being escorted in handcuffs to spend the remainder of his adult life behind bars. What made the situation worse is knowing he will at some point be released to spend some part of his life outside of prison. His much younger foster siblings will not be able to see any of their adult life because scum like him.

The local bar was the usual place where Mr Jackson would spend his nights following shit news. Drinking scotch followed by another and smoking cigars as if they were going out of fashion. The evening normally ended with him taking an escort back to his penthouse apartment and spending the night with them.

Being young and a millionaire, obviously he was an eligible bachelor with lots of women swooning for him. However, he has never had the time to find the right woman. The only person he tends to have the time for, Sammy, his best friend for many years.

Sammy was a black man with loads of potential. He had a child at 17 years old and now spends most of his time raising his son with his ex-girlfriend. However, they do have the odd night out together. Being six years older than Mr Jackson, he was the older brother to him and most of the business ideas came from Sammy with his exceptional business mind. At 19 years old they would have thought that Mr Jackson would have matured by now, taking more of a hands-on approach at the businesses his father left him but instead spent most of his time frittering his money away knowing that in a couple of years he will receive another pay out. Mr Jackson always seemed so resentful towards anything that did not seem justified in the world.

"The money is on the side, usual place," mumbled a hungover Mr Jackson. The scantily dressed lady got out of the bed and headed towards the exit of the penthouse suite.

"You can call me anytime," looking back towards Mr Jackson as she left.

Sammy always said that he needs to find a lady to invest his life in. Always got the same answer, that he has not found the right lady. However, this was about to change at the end of the following week.

"The new administrator starts today, Mr Jackson," explained the manager. She had already made an impression on her fellow colleagues. Turning heads down the corridor. Beautiful, blonde, big breasted and a thirst for hard work.

She waltzed into the office like a catwalk model, holding paperwork and folders and her glasses slipping down her nose. "Hello, I am Kathryn."

"Good morning, I am Mr Jackson." He never spent much time in the office, but he knew from this point that he would be spending more time there. He was a man who knew what he wanted and from this moment he wanted Kathryn.

Chapter 5

"Where are we going, can I open my eyes yet," Kathryn said excitedly. It had only taken Mr Jackson one week to work his magic and he is already on his first date with Kathryn. Flying her to New York City and having a meal at one of the best restaurants in the city, a personal favourite of Mr Jackson.

"You can open your eyes now." Shocked into silence Kathryn was gobsmacked at the effort Mr Jackson went through for her.

"You can order whatever you want," advised Mr Jackson.

"May we have a bottle of champagne and a Scotch please," instructed Mr Jackson.

"This is incredible, never had a first date like this. Thank you," said Kathryn, as they were seated at the table whilst the waiter brought their drinks over.

Mr Jackson never really had a first date, but he knew from the moment he laid eyes on Kathryn, she was the one. He was always going to pull out of the stops.

"Tell me a bit more about yourself," asked Kathryn.

"What would you like to know," asked Mr Jackson.

"I don't know, tell me a bit about you and your family. A backstory of your life," enquired Kathryn.

"You seem mysterious, and I want to know what I am getting involved in."

She was edging closer to the table with starters hovering over her head.

"Starters, sorry for the interruption," mumbled the waiter, as they placed the plates in front of their dining guests.

Mr Jackson had a worried look on his face, knowing he would have to relive some of the memories that have brought trauma to his life. He would do it, as Kathryn was the most beautiful woman he had ever met. He did not want to screw this opportunity up.

His head was swirling as if it was going through a time machine, flashbacks of tragic memories mixed with good times. However, overall, the memories were crappy. The reasons why Mr Jackson was such a complex individual.

"Henry are you OK," a concerned Kathryn asked. It was not often Mr Jackson had been called by his first name. He liked to have that type of authority over people and demanded they call him Mr Jackson, the way a student would call their teacher.

"Yeah, I am fine, just reminiscing about the times in my life where I was happiest. This being one of them. There are not many to be honest," said Henry.

"It started when I was 10 years old. I was brought up quite a privileged child. I was an only child, so my parents tended to get me what I wanted. I know its spoilt but may explain why I usually get what I want now," explained Henry.

"If only it was like that for me, it's understandable. Your parents adored you and as their only child would do anything for you," said Kathryn.

"I was one of five kids, and my parents were the typical blue-collar workers. My dad worked in a steel factory, whilst my Mum spent her time looking after the five of us, followed by a small cleaning job on a night time," Kathryn explaining further.

"You can imagine our household, my parent's wages had to provide for five kids. So, times were hard. This tonight is something I have never been fortunate to witness," said Kathryn. Leaning further in as the starters were taken away. Henry continued with his story.

"One night I heard banging downstairs and as a peered through the banister on the stairway I could see some burglars attacking my parents. Not much later I heard gunshots and just like that my parents were killed," an upset Henry reeled off to Kathryn. Sitting their looking shocked and dismayed. Kathryn could not believe what her date was telling her.

"That is shocking. At ten years old as well. I feel so sorry that you have been going through that nightmare all your life.," Kathryn said.

"Nothing for you to feel sorry for, explained Henry. "It's the fact that one of the offenders only got 30 years. The other only got done for robbery. They both should have been given the death penalty but in my eyes, they have got off scot-free."

She did not really know much about Henry, but Kathryn was started to see a vulnerable and emotional side to him. A complete contrast to the arrogant, egotistical individual who asked her on a date. The main course had only just arrived, and Kathryn had already leaned in for a kiss. Henry reciprocated whether it was sympathy for him after his sob story. Henry did not care he was in love.

"So sorry," Kathryn pushing Henry away. "I was just in the moment."

"Its fine, I have been wanting to do that ever since I met you. You are absolutely beautiful," Henry staring in Kathryn's eyes while praising her. Her come to bed eyes twinkling in a seductive manner.

"I feel like I can just relax around you, Henry," said Kathryn.

"I feel exactly the same, I have never told anyone my feelings regarding my parent's deaths."

Henry continued to absorb Kathryn with his life story.

"I spent most of my teens living with the most amazing foster parents. They understood my circumstances and lived their life around me and my brother and sister," said Henry.

"You have a brother and sister," asked Kathryn.

"Yeah, well a foster brother and sister. I loved them as if they were my actual family. Well, you know what I mean, they were my family but not blood," advised Henry.

"I proved my love and devotion to them when I turned 18. My birthdays were always crap since my parents died but, on my 18th, I inherited everything my parents had."

"Is that why you are in charge of the company and whisking dates off to Michelin star restaurants in New York for their first dates," laughed Kathryn.

"I suppose that is correct but as I mentioned my devotion to my foster parents, I showed this to the point that I gave my foster family a house suitable for their needs," explained Henry.

This one statement made Kathryn look even more lovingly at Henry and now she just wanted to jump all over and rip his clothes off right in the middle of the restaurant. However, she was stopped by Henry's sudden tears.

"What's wrong," a concerned Kathryn asked.

"It was all going well I was finally getting over the death of my parents. I was living their legacy with their inheritance," Henry explained.

"But…" asked Kathryn.

"A fire, massive fire burned my foster family's house to the ground. With them in it. All dead, mum, dad, brother and sister." Henry wiping the tears from his eyes.

"Oh my gosh," an upset Kathryn holding Henry's hand trying to grasp what she heard.

"The worst thing is the bastard only got 25 years in prison. For the second time in my life, justice was not served."

Sammy was the only person Henry had spoken to about his life, however he was is best friend for most of his life. Henry felt a new man when he was around Kathryn.

After the meal, the two of them left and went back to Henry's hotel room. Hand in hand, he was shocked how quickly he had fallen in love with Kathryn. She had a bit of scepticism towards Henry, his inflated ego and money-oriented mind. However, she had seen a new side to him, a more vulnerable and overall decent guy. As they arrived at the entrance to the hotel, Henry looked at Kathryn and thanked her for an amazing evening and apologised for pouring his heart out to her with his depressing past.

Kathryn shook her head and whispered in his ear, "Its ok, you surprised me."

Chapter 6

Kathryn woke up in Henry's hotel room, however she did not feel like one of his one-night stands but felt like a woman in love. Kathryn had boyfriends in past but none of them occurred so quickly after meeting them. With Henry she felt safe and was treated like a princess.

"Morning beautiful, I have some meetings to attend in the city. Get yourself booked into spa and once I have done, we will fly back home," said Henry.

"That would be amazing," said Kathryn.

Kathryn headed to the bathroom to get herself ready for a day of pampering, whilst Henry got his best suit on, for a day of meetings, feeling like a married couple with different daily tasks.

"Start the process of the purchase. I want it," yelled Henry.

Since inheriting his millions, Henry was well known for making extravagant purchases, mainly property.

"There is development happening on it first which may take a few years," the realtor explained.

"I want first refusal of the property as soon as the main work is done," said Henry.

Henry headed out of the room towards the stairs.

"Sir, to confirm we are holding back on the purchase." The assistant asked.

"Yes, I want that main development work done first then as I mentioned I want first refusal. When that work is done, I have more plans," explained Henry.

"I love you," these words had never come out of Henry's mouth before, but he was in love with Kathryn. Back at the hotel, Henry got out of the bath that he shared with Kathryn kissed her on the lips.

"I love you too Henry."

"We will be setting off back to the airport within the hour. I cannot wait to introduce you to my friend, Sammy, "stated Henry.

Kathryn was starting to have doubts that even after one date they were rushing but she had seen a side to Henry that no one had seen before. He had not opened to anybody before. All this trapped trauma has finally come out and given him a new lease of life. He had a spring in his step and new motivation in life to treat Kathryn as the most amazing woman in the world.

After packing their bags, they left the penthouse walked down the long corridor of the hotel, heading outside to Henry's Rolls Royce to his private jet. Is this the life that Kathryn is accustomed to now?

It was only recently she walked into her boss's office as the new administrator now she is jet setting to the greatest city in the world, staying in 5-star luxury as a first date.

"You ok love, you seem a bit quiet," asked Henry. Both sitting there amongst the leather interior of this magnificent car. Far from the lifestyle Kathryn was used to.

"Yeah, I am fine. Just wondering when this all comes out what people at work will think," a panicked Kathryn asked.

Henry holding Kathryn's hand whilst answering her concerns.

"Don't worry about that I am the boss. They do what I say if that is not good enough then there is a nice queue at the unemployment office that they can join."

Defiantly Kathryn looked at Henry.

"I just don't want people thinking I am the office bike, who just sleeps their way to the top. I am a professional who has worked hard all their life."

They were sitting in silence for several minutes taking in what has just been said.

"Don't come into the office then. Do your work from home instead," Henry explaining to a confused Kathryn.

"What do you mean. I cannot just stop coming to the office. That wouldn't look very good."

"Why? I am in charge you can work from wherever you want. I don't want you to feel so cheap. We will make this work." Henry justifying himself with the words, that he does not want to make her feel cheap. This was rich from a guy who slept his way around the city, escort after escort and leaving the measly money on the side. However, the woman sitting next to staring into his eyes, has changed his views on women and life in general. He was no longer the reclusive asshole that he had become since inheriting the family money.

A desperate Henry, holding her hands and looking into a big, beautiful eyes.

"We can make it work," uttered Henry.

"I am not sure Henry, are we rushing into it," a concerned Kathryn with a tear in her eye whispered.

"Don't work at all, I can support you," gasped Henry. At this point there were serious questions that the first real relationship he had was about to end before it had even begun.

"I love you Kathryn, you are the most beautiful woman in the world," Henry declaring to the love of his life. These words the last words mentioned between the two on their way to the airport.

Chapter 7

Henry started to spend less time in the office. They had been dating for three years now and Kathryn was practically reaping the benefits of dating the boss. He would give her his credit card for her to go shopping and pamper days with her friends.

Henry would spend days watching the Major League Baseball followed by drinks at the bar with Sammy, when his best friend was available.

Sammy was going through a tough time with his ex-girlfriend. However, there was another person involved in Sammy's life. Henry had never met them but there were regular fishing trips with the mysterious person. Henry felt pushed out.

"You going to see Sammy today," Kathryn asked.

"Not today, I have errands to run. I should be back this afternoon," explained Henry. Standing up looking very shifty, Henry headed towards the door.

"You're going now, don't you want to have breakfast." Kathryn had started to follow him. Henry looking at Kathryn in the eyes, holding her hand.

"I will try to be quick. Get yourself looking spectacular and I will meet you for dinner," said Henry. A kiss on the lips and Henry had scarpered down the corridor.

"Mate, I am going to ask the big question tonight. Not seen you for a while it would be good to catch up," Henry leaving another voicemail on Sammy's phone.

Henry was getting kind of worried for his friend. For years they were inseparable, the one person Henry could trust and confide in, but he had not seen his lifelong friend for weeks.

Henry started wondering whether this was the time to finally ditch his friend and concentrate on his future with Kathryn. Even though, Sammy was the person there for him when his foster family died. Sammy was the business brains and gave him the advice when it came to the business decisions. Henry taking over a big company at the start of adulthood, the early help from Sammy was invaluable. Sammy was there through all the cheap flings and was over the moon when he finally met Kathryn. He gave his instant approval. Vice versa, Henry was by his friend's side with the trouble Sammy had with his ex-girlfriend, the mother of his child. Joseph, the strapping young lad, 11 years old who in his own eyes Henry treated like a nephew, that was closeness of Henry and Sammy. Just like his dad, Henry had not seen Joseph for weeks either.

Was this the start of his friendship coming to an end and was this a sign to start putting all his energy in his new relationship and hopefully fiancé, Kathryn. Checking his phone to see for any missed calls from Sammy. Nothing. Henry heading back to his apartment with a tear coming down his cheek welling up, with disappointment.

Chapter 8

The sound of waves smashing against the fishing boat, Sammy, and his new friend anxiously wating for the next big catch.

"You fancy a beer my friend, whist we wait," the guy said. Sammy looking down on his phone completely blanking him.

"Sammy, did you hear me," he shouted across the deck of the boat.

"Sorry, just got a lot of my mind," an upset looking Sammy explained.

"I can see that is what's wrong, you don't seem yourself," asked his friend.

"Just got several missed calls and voicemails from Henry but can't seem to listen to them."

"I thought you were keeping your distance. Like I said that guy is bad news for you," said Sammy's friend.

"I know but I feel I need to know what the issue is," a concerned Sammy putting his phone to his ear.

His friend grabbed the phone and launched it into the open sea.

"Why did you do that," shouted Sammy.

"I said we come on these trips to get away from the distractions back home, do you want that beer or not," demanded his friend.

Sammy now looked even more concerned but though what is the point and raised his hand out for the beer.

The beer was going down a bit to well as several cans later the big catch came in.

Even though he was pretty inebriated they managed to pull in the biggest one they have caught for a while.

"Well done," congratulated Sammy's friend.

"Let's go downstairs and celebrate with some stronger stuff."

Heading downstairs with a small bag of white powder and more beers to hand.

Sammy had not done cocaine since he was a teenager, but it was a low point in his life, and this seemed the best way out of it.

It did not take long for Sammy to black out and collapse on the floor. His friend menacingly looking over him.

Sammy gradually coming in and out of consciousness. Eventually woke up.

"I am done now, off to have a nap I think, said Sammy.

"Don't be a party pooper, its only just begun," his friend suggested still with this menacing look in his eyes.

"No, I think I will have a nap and then we can head back to land. I need to see Henry and find out what the issue is." A worried Sammy really at this point felt vulnerable and just wanted to head home.

"We will go when I feel we need to go. It's not often we have a big catch and get chance to celebrate," his friend said as he closely walked towards Sammy.

Chapter 9

"It's him, it's definitely him," the voice echoing in the background. The bright lights and sirens ringing out creating a frantic experience.

It had only been 72 hours, but a body had been found. The one body that he had dreaded to be found.

Henry jolted up, palpations and sweating. Heavy breathing coinciding with disorientation in his face. The lawyer waking Henry up from his sleep, this same nightmare that he was dealing with for past couple of weeks. Seeing his best friend lifted from the sea, dangling there like a piece of meat in a butcher's shop.

"Henry, you were having a nightmare again," the lawyer said to him.

He clearly has not been coping for a while now. That night being the last time seeing his best friend, emerging from the water.

"Today is the day, sir," the lawyer advised.

It wasn't just Henry having issues but 11-year-old Joseph, Sammy's son who was now basically living with Henry. Joseph's Mum (Sammy's ex-girlfriend) had a breakdown and had gone into care. The poor lad had not been to sleep since his dad was reported missing.

As mentioned by his lawyer, the defendant had already agreed a plea bargain for the lesser charge of Voluntary Manslaughter which will stop him getting a life sentence. Henry was fuming after discovering this betrayal of the judicial system.

"I know you feel pissed off that justice is not being served but you need to get ready so we can go to the sentencing," his lawyer explained.

"I just don't understand how someone who obviously was jealous of Sammy's friendship with myself, who clearly planned to murder him can basically get away with the poxy crime of manslaughter," a frustrated Henry shouted.

"I know you have told me but tell me again the ins and outs of it, it is just baffling," said Henry.

His lawyer stood up in front of Henry, Joseph and now Kathryn who had arrived in the room.

The search had already started after Sammy had been reported missing. Jack the suspect had been arrested and was not helping the search whatsoever and was selfishly being a hindrance to the initial case.

After day three of the search they managed to ping and locate Sammy's phone which had been in the sea not far from the body. This helped the investigators to find the body. The police managed to recondition the phone and following further analysis they found several missed calls and voicemails. However, they found one voice mail that had been listened to for about two secs. This potentially was the point before the phone was launched into the sea.

Pathologists found cocaine in Sammy's system which go back to the night that he had gone missing.

Under police interrogation, the suspect already explained that they had beers and cocaine that night. He was jealous of Sammy's friendship and the police believed this was a motive for killing him. However, his lawyers managed to get a plea bargain for voluntary manslaughter and not the more serious crime of 1st degree murder with intent.

Henry had heard this story several times now, but he just wanted to understand how the suspect essentially got off for maliciously killing his best friend.

"Even though he has pleaded guilty, he could still get 20 years," explained his lawyer.

"That does not mean shit, he his young, he can walk out and live outside a free man for the rest of his life. Sammy his dead," an irate Henry shouted.

At this point Joseph burst in into tears knowing his dead won't be coming back. Eyes of anger on Henry's face.

The sound of a gavel slamming down on the desk was becoming a regular occurrence for Henry at this point in his life.

"As you have pleaded guilty, for the crime of Involuntary Manslaughter I sentence you to 20 years in prison," the judge shouted.

"Utter Joke," Henry mumbled under his breath.

"You monster," a teary Joseph shouted towards the dock.

The courtroom went into uproar as the sentenced got escorted out by guards to spend his adult life in prison.

Henry put his arm around Joseph's shoulder.

"I will be there for you for the rest of your life. I will make sure of it," said Henry.

Looking up to him with tears in his eyes, muttered.

"Thank you."

Chapter 10

Henry's priority now was keeping Joseph on the straight and narrow. Even though he was his best friend's son, he was becoming more like his own son.

He signed him up to a prestigious private school to ensure his mind was not on his father's death but on bettering his self-ready for adult life. This was a big step for the normally selfish and self-centred Henry, thinking about someone else first.

Henry still thinks back to that last voicemail he left Sammy that night, the one that was partially listened to by him before his phone had been thrown. Mentioning that he was going to pop the question to Kathryn. He never did in the end there was too much on his mind at the time. Henry was not sure when the right time was now. He loved Kathryn and knew she was the one, but things had changed since Sammy's death and wanted to put all his focus in Joseph.

Henry's long-term plan was when Joseph was old enough, he was going to provide a platform for him, buy him his first house and ensure that he gets a foot in the working world. The worry was that the young lad would end up down the path of depression or mixing with the wrong crowd.

"Enjoy your first day at your new school, Joseph. You will smash it," said Henry.

"I am bit scared, not sure if I am ready," a worried Joseph highlighted. Looking concerned that he would be going to a new environment but without the support of his dad.

Henry knew he was making the right decision sending him to this school. Ensuring he mingles with the right people.

As Joseph headed to school, Henry was quick to leave and head to the bar in the city. The same bar he went to, to get away from his troubles. The bar he went to following the death of his foster family. Now he had purchased the bar and spent even more time there following his recent trauma. One of many businesses in his collection. Kathryn using her relationship with Henry, would do the odd shift behind the bar to have a change of scenery.

"Scotch please, only the one. I am waiting for my son to return home from his first day of school," said Henry.

"What Son, I did not know you had a son Henry," highlighted a punter.

"Well not biological son but a more like a role model. My recently deceased best friend's son." A proud Henry proclaimed.

"What about the mother, they not in the equation," the guy asked.

"No, she recently had a melt down and now gone into a care," explained Henry.

"Well, that's got to be something to celebrate Henry. You don't want just a scotch, let's get a round in, laughed the guy. At this point he had pulled his stool up next to Henry and now acting like they were best buds. Henry with a smirk on his face got the wallet out.

As the day went on, a drunk Henry was pouring his heart out to this customer.

"Henry," shouted Kathryn from across the bar. Heading towards her intoxicated boyfriend.

"You can't keep doing this. Getting smashed as a coping mechanism of your pain you are going through," an upset Kathryn now consoling Henry.

Picking him up from his chair the headed out of the bar.

"Joseph is back from school and waiting for you back at home. I don't think you looking like this is a good impression," said Kathryn.

"Fuck them all, Kathryn. They will all pay for this, shouted Henry. Stumbling more and more as they got into the car.

Kathryn passing some water to Henry put her arms around his shoulders.

"Both you and Joseph are going through the same agony. You both need to sit down and talk to each other. Get a real perspective of what is going on, stated Kathryn.

"I am so sorry," an upset muttered as he turned towards Kathryn.

"I will make sure that I am a better boyfriend to you but also provide that role model support for Joseph," said Henry.

Back at the house, in the bathroom. Joseph looking at his reflection in the mirror wiping away a cut on his cheek. Binning his torn shirt and opening a piece of paper shoved in his bag.

Tears rolling down his eyes as he read the words:
BURN NIGGER

Chapter 11

Life plodded on for Joseph, never telling Henry the truth about the bumps and bruises he regularly got over his body.

They were from playing soccer, was the usual response to the questions from Henry. In theory, the first few months were hell for Joseph. The wrong group of kids constantly belittling him making him feel like dirt.

Joseph would fight back but this would usually make the situation worse. With all what's on his plate, telling Henry the truth would set him back.

Since Sammy's death, Henry was not coping, generally drowning his sorrows with alcohol. Pushing Kathryn away. Which was a shame really, as Joseph had started to get close to Kathryn and since his own mother was unwell, she became like a surrogate mother to him. She knew something was not right with Joseph. She just needed to pinpoint it.

"How was school today," said Kathryn.

"Okay," replied Joseph. Regarding school it only ever was one word answers.

"Any thing interesting in lessons today," asked Kathryn.

"No," replied Joseph.

"Henry has just gone out on some business, he shouldn't be too long," said Kathryn, looking very worried for Joseph.

Joseph headed upstairs desperate to tell the truth of his ordeal at school but deep inside his conscience got the better of him.

Kathryn was tempted to speak to the school but felt it was not her place. Picking up the phone to Henry.

"Hello, we need to talk," Kathryn said down the phone.

Following a half hour chat to Henry, she marched up the stairs to see Joseph.

"Henry is on is way home to talk to you about school," Kathryn explained to Joseph. Who now started to get frustrated with all the questions and probing.

"Nothing is wrong, you stupid bitch, "shouting at Kathryn and slamming the door in her face.

Kathryn was shocked at the attitude of Joseph towards her. She didn't sign up to this. Honestly, Henry didn't either. Deep down though Kathryn knew that the young lad was going through turmoil after the recent death of his father. She knew she had to be there for him and find out exactly what is going on. Heading back downstairs to wait for Henry to arrive home.

Chapter 12

For the next few years Henry and Kathryn tried their best to get Joseph through high school. There were new cuts and bruises and when questioned they would usually get yelled at and doors slammed in their face. However, on the positive side, teacher reports were saying that at school as a whole Joseph was excelling.

But they were concerned about a group of teens that constantly berate Henry. One of the teachers did say they were the well-known troublemakers.

One of them didn't even go to the school and on numerous occasions Joseph was spotted around the school loitering with these gangs. Whether this was an attempt to make friends or was under peer pressure. This would explain these cuts on Joseph's body all the time.

It was not until one evening when Joseph was rushing out from the house, Henry's suspicions were correct.

"Where are you going this time of night," asked Henry.

"Just off to see some friends," replied Joseph in a shifty manner. Knowing something was not right, Henry took his bag off him and looked inside.

Surprisingly there was only a bunch of schoolbooks in the bag.

"Ok don't be too long," said Henry.

Still not convinced, as soon as Joseph left the house, Henry was in pursuit to finally find out was going on.

Upstairs, Kathryn was shocked to find stuffed in the back of Joseph's wardrobe were numerous T-shirts with blood stains on.

One of them spray painted with the words, I AM GOING TO KILL YOU NIGGER.

Running down the stairs to show henry her discovery, but she was too late.

An hour later, Henry came through the door.

"I couldn't find him Kathryn. I am worried something bad is going on with Joseph," said Henry.

Kathryn handed Joseph the T-shirts.

"This will show your worries are right. I think he is being bullied in a bad way," said Kathryn.

Opening the T-Shirt to read the words.

Henry picked up his phone.

"We need to call the police and tell them our worries," said Henry.

Chapter 13

There was a knock on the door. Henry went to answer.
"Mr Jackson," the officer said.
"At last, we rang ages ago. To report a missing child but also to discuss a potential assault of this child," replied Henry.
"Are you the guardian of Joseph," said the officer.
"I am, yes," a worried Henry answered the officer.
"I have some bad news. Joseph was stabbed tonight by another teenager who we have already located and taken in for questioning," said the officer.
"Oh my god is he okay," asked Henry as he was putting his coat back on.
"He was taken to hospital and died when he got there. I am so sorry," said the officer.
Henry barged past the officer with a crying Kathryn in tow.

Driving like a maniac down the highway, with his head all over the place.
"Henry slow down or we will be dead too," screamed Kathryn.

"I can't, I need to see him. It's all my fault. If only I stopped him going out tonight," cried Henry.

"It's not your fault," said Kathryn.

They pulled up at the hospital and asked for which room. Henry ran down the corridor and into the room.

"No, No, No," he shouted.

Henry knelt next to the bed holding Joseph's hand.

"I promised I would look after you and I failed. I am sorry. Please forgive me Joseph," wept Henry.

Kathryn pulled him away from the bed so the doctors can move him.

Kathryn and Henry embraced whilst watching Joseph being wheeled away.

Chapter 14

It was very much back to the old ways of Henry. Drinking all day and all night. He could not bear to help plan the funeral. This was a lot harder than previous funerals that Henry has attended.

Joseph had so much potential, and he was struck down in his prime by a racist thug. Henry beating himself up over it. Believing he could have done more not just that night but in his life in general.

"Last Orders" the bartender shouted across the bar. Henry was stumbling to the bar to get his final orders in.

"Not serving you anymore Mr Jackson," the bartender said.

Henry stuttering and struggling to get his words out, collapsed to the floor.

Henry waking up next morning in his bed with Kathryn sitting next to him.

"Henry, you need to stop the drinking. You are just self-harming yourself," said Kathryn.

Henry siting up with tears rolling down his face.

"Everybody who gets close to me die. How do you think that feels," said Henry.

"I am here for you Henry. I am not going anywhere," replied Kathryn.

"I wouldn't get too close to me, or you will be next. Look at my life. My parents are dead, my foster parents are dead. My best friend is dead and a kid who was like a son to me is now dead," said Henry.

Kathryn who was now welling up felt so sorry for him.

"You need to get out of this bed. Get your best suit on and get back to work. You need a proper distraction," said Kathryn.

Henry now standing up and looking at himself in the mirror.

"When you look at yourself now Henry. Do you see a successful businessman with a loving girlfriend by his side. Or do you see a down an out loser who is just feeling sorry for himself," said Kathryn.

"I don't know. I just see a guy who has ruined his life and has no body left in this world," said Henry.

"Excuse me. You have me," responded Kathryn.

"You get yourself ready, go to work as tomorrow you will be attending the funeral. After that you will go to the court case to see that racist thug get sent down," dictated Kathryn now pulling a suit out of the wardrobe.

"Okay," Henry replied as he slowly got ready for the day.

Chapter 15

He had only just attended the funeral of Joseph last week. Henry was still heartbroken. For him it was like losing a son. That's what he has been to him for the past few years. Henry was beginning to think he was cursed. Everyone close to him has died. The court date had arrived and the idea seeing the racist sent to prison was only thing keeping him going.

As a juvenile the prosecutors were not confident, he would get a long sentence. Heading into the court room arm in arm with Kathryn waiting to see the fate of his son's murderer.

"As the defendant is 16 and has shown remorse over his actions, I will be taking this into consideration," the judge proclaimed.

There were boos from the court room as the judge continued with his speech.

"However, this was a hate crime. A murder of another juvenile because they were black," said the judge

All these recommendations aside, I believe the most fitting sentence for this crime is…15 years. With the first couple of years spent in Youth detention centre," said the judge as the gavel went down.

Henry fuming went to attack the parents of the defendant before being escorted out by security. Kathryn quickly followed.

Outside the courthouse Henry approached the parents of the defendant again. Kathryn trying her best to pull him back.

"Your son will not get away with this. I will make sure his life inside is hell," shouted Henry. The parents rushed away into a taxi.

"You need to calm down Henry. Before you get yourself arrested," said Kathryn.

"Screw this and the legal system," yelled Henry has he headed away from the courthouse.

Kathryn was worried what he would do. The poor guy can't get break, and everything seems to collapse around him.

Chapter 16

"Happy Birthday to you. Happy Birthday to you. Happy Birthday to Henry. Happy Birthday to you," the whole room cheered. Henry celebrating his birthday with some of his work colleagues and Kathryn.

It had been a crap five years since Joseph's death to the hands of the racist thug. However, a milestone birthday spent with Kathryn was something to kind of be happy about.

"Thank you all for coming it means a lot. As you are aware I have had a tough time recently but spending my birthday with you lot means a lot and as brought a smile on my face," said Henry to his party guests. Raising a glass to his friends.

"Let's all get drunk," smiled Henry.

The party was in full swing, Henry chatting away to some of his business associates. This allowing Kathryn to slope off for a cigarette.

Once outside with cigarette to the mouth, a big sigh from Kathryn.

"Oh, that is bliss," she said.

She started to hear some rustling nearby. Getting quite frightened she started to put her cig out. There was a guy standing in the darkness at the end of the alleyway staring at her. Long hair, ripped clothes looked like he was high on drugs, started to approach her. Scared for her safety Kathryn rang back inside to rejoin the party.

"You ok love," asked Henry. Kathryn looking quite shaken.

"Yeah, I am fine. Just a creepy guy outside scared me whilst I was getting some fresh air. I am ok now though," replied Kathryn.

"Let's go get drink and forget about it," said Henry.

The clock had nearly struck midnight and the shots were still being passed around. At this point Henry was inebriated sitting in the corner. Chatting and sharing Scotch with one of the managers of his company.

Kathryn was drunk herself stumbling towards the toilets.

"You ok Kathryn. Do you need some help," one of the fellow guests asked.

"Nah. I am fine. Just going outside for some fresh air," mumbled Kathryn.

Kathryn standing in the same alleyway that gave her the creeps earlier that evening and putting a cigarette in her mouth.

"You got a light," a voice in the darkness said.

Kathryn not realising what she was doing, turned around to give this stranger a light. From the darkness the same guy from before approached her.

He pulled a knife on her and grabbed her by the hands.

"You scream bitch, and I will kill," the guy shouted.

"What do you want. I can give you money," said Kathryn. In tears giving him her handbag.

"I don't want your handbag. I want you," the guy now grabbing her face with his hands reaching for her crotch.

"Pants down now," he yelled at her.

Kathryn kneed him in the stomach but as she tried to escape, she tripped. The guy even more angry picked her up and punched her in the face forcing her to the ground. Using his knife, he slit her face followed by him forcing his tongue down her throat. Using his knife again, he now ripped her pants off.

"Shut up you bitch and hold still," he muttered into her ear. Kathryn lying there like a corpse feeling worthless.

"Have you seen Kathryn," Henry asked one of the guests.

"I last saw her heading outside for some fresh air. I have not seen her come back in since though," the guest replied. Looking concerned, Henry stumbling his way through the guests headed outside.

Once outside Henry rushed over to Kathryn who was sitting there in tears, pants ripped and round her ankles.

"Oh my god. Kathryn what happened," shouted Henry.

"I couldn't do anything. I was just lying there," sobbed Kathryn. Her tears down her face now mixing with the blood for the knife wound and the rain that had started to fall.

"I couldn't do anything," Kathryn repeated. Henry was on the phone to the police at this point whilst, consoling Kathryn.

"I just couldn't do anything," said Kathryn once again.

Chapter 17

Kathryn didn't turn up for the sentencing. The experience was too raw for her. However, her testimony and the evidence provided to the jury, the prosecutors believed was enough to send the guy down for life. They had already got the guilty outcome for rape.

Henry as usual hired the best lawyers in town and was happy that the prosecutors are going for maximum sentence. Henry entered the courtroom to hear the sentencing. Experience showed, Henry never got the outcome that was deserved. This would feel like a stab in the back from the justice system that his fiancé who was aggressively raped and left sitting in an alleyway with blood from her face and bruises over her body.

Henry sitting there in the stands watching the proceedings take place. The judge explaining the charge that the defendant had previously been found guilty for.

The judge got everyone's attention and Henry sitting there with his eye shut and fingers crossed. Waiting to hear the life sentence being handed out.

The gavel slammed on the desk.

"I sentence you to serve a maximum of 18 years," ordered the judge.

Henry looked up in disgust.

"You have got to be kidding me," shouted Henry. Looking towards Kathryn's lawyers who were so confident he would get life in prison.

Henry charged out of the courtroom in anger and frustration knowing that the guy who raped his fiancé could be back on the streets in less than 18 years.

One of the lawyers caught up with Henry in the hallway.

"We tried our best. I am sorry," said the lawyer

"Henry, we can appeal the sentence if you want," explained the lawyer.

"What is that going to do. You were confident that he would get life in prison. Now the sick bastard will be released in the future and who is to say that he won't attack again, "said Henry.

"Don't worry about it. You guys are fired. I will sort this out myself," a disgusted Henry explained to a now shocked lawyer as he walked away from the courthouse.

Chapter 18

The plates smashed against a kitchen wall. Once again, a drunken Henry furious since last week's verdict. Every day since, he has been going out getting intoxicated taking frustrations out on Kathryn.

"How can he basically get away with it. After what he did to you," shouted a frustrated Henry. Now getting closer and closer to Kathryn. A scared Kathryn stepping back in worry.

"You have said this every day since that night. I can't do this anymore." An annoyed Kathryn headed up stairs. Henry chucking a plate towards the door as she left.

"Where are you going," yelled Henry as he grabbed Kathryn's arm.

"Get off me, you are hurting me," Kathryn trying to pull him off.

"I am off to my counselling session. I can't cope with this today," said Kathryn.

"When are you back," asked Henry. Now releasing Kathryn but looking more annoyed that the one person left in his life, he feels he is losing.

"I will be gone all day," said Kathryn.

As soon as the door shut, Henry was on the phone.

"Are you coming over. Usual price," said Henry.

It had taken half an hour and Henry's prostitute had arrived. Kathryn went to counselling whilst Henry's coping mechanism was having affairs and drinking.

"Money is on the side, see you again soon," said Henry. The scantily clad woman scurried away but leaving the bedroom. The front door went.

"Henry I am back, we need to talk," shouted Kathryn from bottom of stairs.

"Oh shit," yelled Henry jumping out of bed. However, it was too late.

"Who are you," Kathryn could be heard saying to the woman.

She ran out of front door at the same time Kathryn was making her way up the steps.

"Don't you dare say anything," Henry abruptly said to Kathryn. In shock though, Kathryn replied with a bit of sympathy over the situation.

Kathryn headed towards the bed and sat next to Henry, holding his hand.

"It is hard I understand. We have not been the same since that night," said Kathryn who now had tears in her eyes.

The anger in Henry turned to a more empathic feeling. Knowing he needed to provide more support to his girlfriend.

Putting his arm around her, he whispered.

"I am sorry."

"I don't think we can go on like this. You clearly can't get over the sentencing that was passed down. I have suffered much worse with the rape and all it has been about is you. You are wanting revenge," said Kathryn as she explained her true feelings towards Henry.

"That's not true," replied Henry.

"It would be best if we go our separate ways. I need to move back to my family, who have been so supportive over all of this," said Kathryn gradually moving Henry's arm from around her.

Jumping up and grabbing Kathryn by the hair.

"You stupid bitch, you are not going anywhere," shouted Henry.

"Get off me you are hurting me," screamed Kathryn as she was chucked to the wall banging her head in the process.

"I had a surprise for you tonight, a place for us to forget our problems but you have ruined that," yelled Henry menacingly looking at Kathryn.

"Get the hell out of my house you stupid whore." Henry barging his way out of the bedroom.

Kathryn holding her head and startled as she heard a thud of the front door.

Tears coming down her eyes feeling like her life is meaningless.

Chapter 19

"Mr Jackson, can we see you today about the offer you have put in." The voice over the phone was trying to urgently get this information through to Henry but this time in the morning he was hungover, the phone hanging from his ear.

"Call me back later," Henry replied and dropping the phone to the bed.

This time there were two lady friends who provided entertainment for him last night. Being a rich, powerful individual, he has always felt he can do what he wants and get away with it.

It had only been a matter of hours after breaking up with the only woman he has truly loved, and he was back to his old ways.

"Ladies please, it is time to go now. I have some urgent business I have to attend."

Henry stumbling out of bed and into the bathroom.

Looking into the mirror and shouting back into the room.

"The money is on the side, help yourself."

The ladies at his point we're getting themselves ready and heading out.

"Nice to see you again Mr Jackson," one of the ladies shouted back.

Henry was far too hungover to even acknowledge what they were saying. Back in the bedroom he collapsed onto the bed.

A couple of days had past and Henry was now in a much better state to deal with business.

"As my identification passed. This is a fresh start for me, and I want my past basically erased," Henry pleading with the person on the phone.

Henry was back to being the demanding businessman he was known for. The two day bender is behind him, and changes were starting to be made in his life.

"All done now. All checked out," the voice on the phone advised.

"Good. I must go now, I am heading to my office to speak to my realtor send the paperwork over to them now. Thank you," Henry replied.

Henry heading out of his apartment, down the elevator and into his chauffeur driven car.

Arriving at his office an excited, smartly dressed individual approached Henry, pouncing on him as soon as he stepped out of the car.

"Congratulations the deposit has been paid and your purchase of the private island has gone through, Mr…Jackson, is it," the realtor said.

"I go by my birth name now; you can use that. It is Newman, Walter Newman.

Chapter 20
Newman Cay

Sitting in his office on his island, all those distressing memories in his life that he thinks and looks back on every day of his complicated life. The trauma he must deal with every day. Walter had never conveyed these stories back to anyone before, but Dan with tears coming down his eyes, now understood why Walter Newman is understandably a loner and as a sense of psychopath in him.

"I can't believe the life you have had," Dan upsettingly said to Walter. "Now I totally understand why you have been behaving the way you have for all these years sir."

Dan never really paid much attention to the newspaper cut outs on the office wall, that Walter constantly stands and stares at. However now it all makes sense.

The headlines and snippets of the newspaper cut outs on the wall read as the following:

ARSON ATTACK KILLS 4
25 Years for attacker.
Was justice served?

DRUGGED, DROWNED AND LEFT TO DIE

HATE CRIME ON THE STREETS
Kid stabbed because of the colour of his skin.

DOUBLE MURDER
10-Year-old boy left an Orphan following robbery and double murder.
Life in prison for the killer.

RAPE SUSPECT SENTENCED TO 18 YEARS

These were the exact events in his life that caused Walter so much distress and anger. That is why he picked five ex-prisoners to join him on his tropical island. Five crimes and five people. He felt justice had not been served, he wanted to punish somebody. Walter wanted retribution.

Dan understood Walter but looked quite scared what Walter had in store for these prisoners. It was not a rehabilitation holiday what these prisoners thought they were getting.

"Wait till tomorrow comes along," explained Walter. With a creepy smile on his face.

"My guests have enjoyed the first couple of days. Let them relax, so they feel like they are having a break. As once that is over, they are in for a shock of their life," laughed Walter.

"Sir, I understand what you have been through but please don't do something you will regret," a concerned Dan begged is boss.

"You know me Dan, I don't regret things in my life. I do things to enhance my emotions and improve myself." Walter with a hand on Dan's back.

"Get yourself back to your room and I will see you bright and early my friend," said Walter.

Dan looking more scared and concerned with the situation, headed out of the office, took one last look behind to Walter. Currently, he was looking out of window to the beach of his tropical paradise.

Still looking out of the window reminiscing about his life, feeling like he has got his problems of his life off his chest. Now however, Walter was concerned that he had told his one trusted confidante too much information. He has seen the newspaper cut outs; he now knew his life of trauma.

It was now best to keep the rest of his plans too himself until the last minute. Dan knew his task for tomorrow, that is all he must do. Walter would do the rest.

"Mother and father. The Jacksons. Sammy, Joseph, and Kathryn. I will get justice for you all. I promise," Walter mumbled to himself with a smirk on his face, looking down watching is unwitting guests.

Chapter 21

Dan had been up since the sun was rising this morning. He had been checking up on the guests all day ensuring they were being catered for.

"Afternoon Jason," said Dan. At this point Jason looked less of the homeless tramp with a beard, he looked like when he arrived. He had shaved ready for the meal tonight.

Continuing is walk around the island greeting and checking up on the guests. All this while Walter watching from above in his office with a big cigar in his mouth.

A helicopter landed on the island and the passenger on board was swiftly taken to Walter's office. Guests landing on the island never really passed Dan's mind, but this guest grabbed his attention more than others. He was wearing a suit carrying a bag and the speed he was whisked to Walter's office was interesting.

Dan at this point looked up at Walter's office but he had now drawn the curtains, increasing his curiosity.

It had only been 20 minutes at most before the man had come back out and heading back to the helicopter. This time he had a briefcase which only Dan can assume was full of money.

Dan had seen this type of transaction before so was used to seeing different people leaving Walter's office with a briefcase full of money.

Dan reminded the guests to be ready and at the main complex on the southern part of the island, for the welcome dinner.

The guests after being reminded were hurrying back to their rooms to get ready. Dan was heading towards the southern part of the island. However, whilst heading there he had not realised that the building which has been under construction for the past several weeks and only a few days ago had scaffolding on it, was no longer being refurbished. Completely going over Dan's head, showing how busy and distracted he has been recently.

He had arrived at the main complex with the table all set out. The guests started to hurtle through the door.

"Please take a seat anywhere, apart from the end chairs," laughed Dan. They were big, tall chairs running alongside a long table where the guests could comfortably sit around.

"Please sit down," a voice shouted. Walter appeared from the darkness to join his guests at the table.

"Drinks were brought to the guests as soon as they sat down.

"The drinks I have picked for you are the ones from your preference sheets when you arrived. Can we all make a toast, to great friends and family," said Walter. Dan looked over to him and could see a devious smile from his evil face.

Dan knew from this point these guests were in trouble but did not know how.

The guests were tucking away into their three-course meal made up of starter, main meal, and a dessert to finish. A couple of hours had past until Walter stood up.

"Can I have your attention; we do not have long. I hope you are enjoying your meal," shouted Walter, as the guests stopped and stared.

"I am Walter, owner of Newman Cay." Walter standing there arrogantly proud of himself.

"You have all been brought here. As you all have one thing in common. You are all scum of the world," said Walter.

"Screw you," Cameron the youngest out of the guests shouted.

The guests now looking incensed, but this did not bother Walter as he continued to heckle his guests.

"You are all ex-prisoners, each of you committing horrible crimes. The problem is each of these crimes had a massive impact on my life.

Dan's ears now pricked up looking very intrigued.

"Let's start with you then Cameron, since you are being so vocal," said Walter. Cameron now standing up from his chair.

"You stabbed a young black kid when you were younger in a racially motivated attack. No wonder you have that horrible tattoo on your face, that basically sums you up. Horrible racist"

Cameron jumped across the table towards Walter but was restrained by the other guests.

"The issue we have with that Cameron is that young kid was like a son to me. The reason for that was that his father was killed by him," Walter shouted as he turned his head towards Jack. The prisoner sitting opposite Cameron.

"Poor old Jack here, drugged and drowned my lifelong best friend and left him to die." Walter staring with anger in Jack's face.

Jack stood up now and looked apologetic for his actions.

"No wonder he is afraid of water," Walter proclaimed.

Walter continued to berate his guests and now turned his attention to the person sitting next to Jack.

"Jason, you were the first guest to arrive and why don't we tell your fellow guests what you did."

Walter now getting more and more worked up.

"This sick man killed my foster family in an arson attack. He said it was because he was drunk, but it is because he is an evil son of a bitch, Walter shouted with more intent.

Dan held back Jason before he ran towards Walter to punch him.

"The truth hurts doesn't it," Walter said.

"Now we turn to Damian. I would say he is the lowest of the lot. He raped my fiancé. The love of my life." Walter knew this would hurt Damian. He always thought rape was the worst crime out of them all.

"Finally, we have Eli. I have left you till the end because this hurt me the most. You were the scum bag who orphaned me at ten years old. Killing my mother and father."

Eli made a big gulp whilst Dan looked over in shock. Now knowing this was Walter's full plan all along to get revenge. Dan now visibly seeing the guests looking dazed and stuttering around.

"As part of your meal, what I have done is drugged you with a powerful medicine called Selerodine Neutroloxin." Walter with a sadistic smile on his face explaining to his now confused dinner guests.

"What this does is it will paralyse your nerves and you will fall asleep within two hours of receiving the drug. This was approximately one hour and fifty-five minutes ago," laughed Walter whilst lighting a cigar.

"In the next five minutes you will all collapse on the floor and fall asleep. In the morning you will wake up not remembering much what happened, but you will realise that this is not the rehabilitation holiday you think it is, but it is my game. I feel that I did not get the justice that was deserved following the horrible crimes you all committed. I believe in eye for an eye when it comes to punishment. I believe in proper payback," said Walter.

At this point, each of the prisoners were one by one slowly keeling over onto the floor.

"Gentlemen, I would like to wish you all good night," said Walter.

"Welcome to Retribution Island."

Chapter 22

"What the hell," shouted Jason.

"Someone help me." Looking behind, hearing chains rattle against a bed.

"What kind of sick game is this," a panicked Jason trying to rag the chains off their connection.

"I am sorry," a desperate Jason sobbing wondering what was going on. All he remembers was eating dinner last night and now he is tied to a bed.

Dan rampaging around his room after the worse night sleep of his life. He was wondering what to do. He could call the police, but they may think he was part of this terrible game which his boss thought was pleasurable.

Only one thing for him to do was to leave the island as soon as possible, preferably without seeing Walter. He couldn't wait around and see what Walter had in store for his prisoners.

"Help me," Jason continued to shout in desperation running out of energy after spending last 15 minutes trying to break free from these chains.

"Good morning, Jason," a voice could be heard over a speaker.

"Let me go, you asshole," Jason pleading with the voice he can hear above him.

"Now that you are awake you are now part of the game," the voice now Jason knew was Walter's said in a sadistic manner.

"What game is this. You're a sick freak," Jason yelled now with anger in his voice.

"As a mentioned in front of the other guests. You killed my foster family by setting their house on fire. The house I gifted them, for everything they have done for me," highlighted Walter.

"I am so sorry, I was drunk. Why do you think I don't drink anymore? I couldn't live with the guilt," a sobbing Jason said.

"Lies," shouted Walter.

"You used that as an excuse. You did it as you are a horrible human being," said Walter.

"Me, horrible. Look what you are doing to me," Jason mentioned in his defence.

Jason now continued to rag the chains off but with little success.

"As I now have your attention. If you didn't behave like a caged animal, you would have noticed that the key for the lock on the chains is hanging on the wall next to you." Jason now turning to his right as Walter explained this.

"At the bottom of the bed there is a stick looks like a broomstick, but it has a hook on it. Luckily, with all the kicking and screaming, you haven't knocked it off the bed," said Walter.

Jason now looking around to see what else there was.

" I have only tied your arms up as I want to give you the chance to free yourself." Walter now highlighting that not putting chains on Jason's leg was all part of the plan.

Jason started to smell a very distinctive smell.

"I am glad you have noticed the smell. That smell is gasoline which has been poured around the room," Walter started to laugh.

Heavy breathing from Jason. With a worried look in his face started to beg. This was to no avail, as Walter continued to explain his plan.

"You have ten minutes to let yourself free from the chains. My suggestion is to use your feet to grab the stick and try and hook the keys off the wall," said Walter.

At this point Jason had already started to attempt to grab the stick.

"However, if you drop the keys as you are lifting, personally that makes it pretty hard for you." Walter with a sadistic laugh using Jason as a pawn in his game.

"What happens if I manage to get free," asked Jason.

"Well, the door to the room is unlocked and you will be free to go," Walter highlighted in response to Jason's question.

"Don't forget as I mentioned last night. I believe in eye for an eye in crime punishment. If you don't get out in ten minutes, then I will set the room on fire and in my calculation the entire room will be burnt down including yourself in about 1 minute from ignition." Walter now confidently saying.

"You sick bastard, let me go," Jason yelled without success.

"Good luck. Your time starts now," shouted Walter

Dan still debating his options ahead of him. If he stays the police arrest him as part of the plan but if he leaves then he would be looking over his shoulder for the rest of his life wondering what Walter would do to him, because of his betrayal.

Dan picked the latter. Starting to pack his bags ready to get the hell of this island.

First, he needed some cash and transport off this island.

"Nearly, nearly," panting with every effort, Jason using the stick trying to hook the keys, his legs stretched out.

"Shit," shouted Jason. The keys dropping to the floor and time running out. Jason knew this was his life coming to an end.

The sound of a timer bellowed out and a flash occurring. Flames blasting through the room. Jason staring at the flames

"Sorry," were his last words.

Chapter 23

"Anyone there. What is going on," shouted Jack.

Stranded in a cage above the sea. Ten foot above the water and 50 feet from the shore. Jack knew no one could hear him.

Dan now with his duffle bag of clothes looked out of his window and could see Jack screaming for help.

His conscience wanted to go and help but that makes him involved.

He had one thing on his mind he needed cash to get off this island. He knew Walter's office was full of cash, he just needs to get there. With his duffle bag over his shoulder headed out of his villa complex. Trying to mask out the shouts of help coming from the sea.

"Can someone tell me what is going on," yelled Jack. Him now looking very concerned. One moment he was enjoying a nice meal and now he has woken up in a cage above the Caribbean Sea.

Jack could see a speaker in the cage, and it started crackling.

"Hello Jack," the voice muttered.

"Like I mentioned yesterday this is my game. Eye for an eye," Walter's voice clearly explaining the scenario.

Jack shaking the cage, trying to escape but with no luck. Looking more and more scared.

"As you know, I didn't bring you to this island on a rehabilitation holiday. This is my game, and you are my next player," Walter started laughing down the speaker even louder.

"What the hell do you want from me. Please just let me go I am sorry for what I did," a desperate Jack begging to be let go.

"Below as you know is the Caribbean Sea." Walter explaining to an angry Jack.

"No shit sherlock," shouted Jack at the speaker now shaking the cage to the point it was swinging side to side.

"Let me finish as this will be the difference between life and death. You have ten minutes to get out of the cage." Walter clearly explains to Jack.

Jack now looking more and more interested, knows there is a chance to get off this island alive.

"On top of the roof of the cage, there is a hacksaw. This can cut the metal poles off the cage. However, the longer you take the blunter it will become and overall make it harder for you to cut the poles." Walter laughed down the speaker with his evil laugh.

"I reckon about three poles you could squeeze through and drop down into the sea. I hope you can swim as you are still 50 feet from the shore," said Walter.

"Is that it. Then I can leave." Jack finding this hard to believe but knew he must take part in this twisted game.

"Yep. However, as I mentioned you have ten minutes and in that time the cage will be lowered into the sea. After that if you have not escaped by then, my calculations are that you will last about one minute before you drown," Walter's laugh getting even more evil.

"You are sick," a shocked Jack gasped.

"You will then know what it was like for my best friend, when you drugged him, drowned him and left him to die," roared Walter.

"You have ten minutes and hopefully you will suffer the same as him," chuckled Walter.

Dan now arrived in Walter's office luckily had not been spotted by anyone.

Rifling through the drawers of his desk not finding anything. He needed cash. Something Dan knew Walter had lots of but needed to locate it.

Heading back down the corridor towards the library. He could see through the glass, Walter sitting there talking to a screen.

"What is he doing," Dan whispered to himself.

Dan ducking before Walter could see him. Opened the door of the library and went towards a specific bookshelf. This bookshelf was of significance to Dan for many years. He knew there was money stashed somewhere.

Taking a few books off the shelf.

"There it is," said Dan. In front of him was a box. Opening the box and there was a stash of notes, must have been thousands of dollars. Grabbing a handful of the cash and shoving in his duffle bag. Dan ran back out of the library. Next step was getting off the island. Walter had a personal helicopter which could be ready for transporting him and anyone on the island at any time of day. Just needed to get the message sent to them.

However, in the back of his mind he was still contemplating calling the police. Oblivious to the fact that one of the guests had burnt to death and the other was close to drowning.

"Fuck. One more should do it," Jack was knackered, gasping for air whilst still trying to hacksaw these metal poles away.

The time running out, water was on the floor of the cage.

"Walter. I am sorry," yelled Jack.

The cage came to a sudden stop, swaying on the surface of the water. Jack looking up wondering what was going on.

"Jack you actually said sorry again," said Walter over the speaker.

"I really am," Jack wondered now if the game was up and he would be spared from death.

"You were not willing to take your proper punishment. You murdered Sammy but you were only given manslaughter charges. I want you to admit you killed my best friend in cold blood. Then I may consider letting you go." Walter with an unconvincing tone to his voice but Jack at this point would take anything to escape. He had only managed to saw off two metal poles, but his hacksaw was now blunt.

Jack now staring at the speaker.

" Walter, I am sorry

I killed Sammy. I was jealous of his friendship with you. I wanted him to myself and was trying to take him away from you," said Jack. Instantly the cage lowered at a double the speed.

The sea splashing, the cage now submerged under the water.

" Asshole," the last word heard over the speaker.

" What the hell," Dan, who at this point looked out of the window into the distance could see a splash in the sea. He knew that was Jack.

Chapter 24

"At least five have been killed. Newman Cay Island. There could be more." Dan had made the call. Help was on its way. He needed to get away as soon as possible.

Waking up in a dingy cellar it was pitch black, a very pungent smell.

"Hello," a voice shouted through the darkness.

Suddenly a light switched on. Cameron on his knees wondering what the hell was going on.

"Anybody there," he shouted once again but now he knew there was no one else in the room.

"Welcome Cameron," a voice in a speaker from above bellowed to him whilst he was crouching on the floor.

"Who is that what do you want," said Cameron as he finally stood up to get closer to the voice he could hear from the speaker.

"You are my next player of the game," the voice got louder.

"Walter is that you, what is the problem with you." Cameron looking frustrated knowing the situation he was in was out of his hands.

"If you look to the wall, they are covered in knives," explained Walter.

Cameron looking around with a shocked look on their face.

"However, I will give you the opportunity to escape. Also, if you notice in between the occasional knife, there is a stone."

Cameron paying close attention to the positions of these stones. Knowing that there is a possibility of escape. Looking up there was a door at the top.

"As you have just noticed there is a door which is unlocked at the top." Walter now with a smug voice down the speaker.

"You have ten minutes. However, during this time, the walls will gradually move towards each other and if you run out of time you will be crushed and stabbed to death by the knives. Exactly what happened to poor Joseph because of your racist actions," shouted Walter now even more angry.

"You are a horrible racist, you put his life through hell. You finished him off by racially stabbing him to death and I want you to suffer just like he did."

"I am sorry. I am a changed person. Prison made me a more considerate human being. Please, I don't want to play this game." Cameron trying to plead with Walter.

"Tough. The walls are now moving," shouted Walter. As Cameron headed towards the first stone on the wall, the walls were slowly moving towards him.

Chapter 25

The sound of dripping water, mixed with crying echoing in the warehouse style room.

"Help. Somebody help me," a sobbing Damian.

"Please." Damian lying there on a table like a piece of meat in an abattoir.

Legs wide open with his privates dangling freely, a metre above a table saw.

"What the fuck," shouted Damian. Lying there with his penis hanging out, legs and arms tied to a table, absolutely humiliated.

Walter watching on a camera with a perverted smile on his face. Watching the ultimate humiliation of his next prisoner.

"Is anyone there, what the hell is going on," Damian continued shouting. Struggling to release himself from the shackles.

"What sick freak would do this," cried Damian.

Now a voice could be heard over the speaker.

"It is not nice, is it," the voice said.

"Who is that" a startled Damian turned towards the voice.

"It's not nice being left in such a vulnerable, humiliating position," the voice said. Continuing to heckle Damian, lying there half naked begging to be released.

"Let me go. What is wrong with you," shouted Damian.

"I said you will wake up not remembering what happened. Did you enjoy your meal," Walter now laughing.

"Walter, what is your problem," screamed Damian. Using all the strength he had left to try to break free.

"You. You are the problem. The lowest scum of the world. You make me sick." Walter now getting frustrated.

"You like games, don't you Damian?"

"Fuck you and fuck your stupid games," screamed Damian.

"That's a shame. I was going to give you the opportunity to escape," stated Walter.

Damian now listening in interest in what Walter had to say. Panic and fear displaying on his face but intrigued as there was a possibility of escape.

Damian was always dubious about taking part in this program. When he got the call, he felt that it was too good to be true. Now he knew he was right in the end. His life hanging in the balance.

"What I fancy doing for the next ten minutes is leave you lying there naked, like the piece of shit you are. Humiliation at its best," proclaimed Walter.

"What happens after ten minutes. Will you let me go," asked Damian.

"I might do, but you have to tell me what exactly happened that night you raped Kathryn. I want to hear everything," said Walter.

Whilst you are doing this, a saw will move closer to your privates and if I hear any bullshit. I will not stop it and it will rip your penis to pieces.

A shocked look descended on Damian's face.

At the same time, with time going against him. Cameron near the top of the wall and knew the end was near.

"Shit," shouted Cameron, as he slipped down the wall. All the hard work gone. Quickly adjusting himself and ascending the wall once again.

Feeling the knives pressing against his back, from the wall behind. Time was up. He was crushed, knives stabbing through every part of his body.

Chapter 26

Dan was making his way towards Walter's office and heard a gunshot followed by a scream.

Another gunshot followed quickly after. Turning back Dan headed towards the sound to see who it was and what was going on.

The ten minutes was not even up before Walter pulled the trigger on Damian. He could not stand the thought of this low life of a person ever leaving this island alive.

Walter now leaving his vantage point with the gun by his side headed to another room. Satisfied with today's work, Walter swung open the door and came face to face with his last prisoner, his nemesis, the first person who he ever hated.

"Eli. How are we doing?" said Walter.

Dan arrived at the room where the gun shot came from.

Throwing up after witnessing the scene. Blood everywhere and a naked body lying there on a table.

Turning away from the murder scene, Dan didn't want to get involved. He was going to leave it for the authorities to deal with when they arrive.

Eli was standing at the other side of the room chained to the wall but looking directly at Walter, who was stood at the entrance to the room.

"Why did you do it. I was ten years old. You left me an orphan. Over a bit of money was it," yelled Walter.

"It was more than money. I despised your father. He screwed me over and I wanted revenge," said Eli.

With eyes now bulging and anger in his face, Walter clenched his gun.

"Your father was not the saint you thought he was. He was a bad man. I worked for him, and he backstabbed me in a deal and left me broke. I was just getting back what I was owed," explained Eli.

"My mother she did nothing to me. I was ten years old, and I witnessed both my parents being killed," shouted Walter coming ever closer to Eli.

"Honestly, I didn't know he had kids therefore was unaware you were there. For you mother, she was just in the wrong place at the wrong time," laughed Eli.

Walter holding the gun to Eli's head foaming from the mouth.

"Go on then shoot me, I don't give a shit. Let's be honest though, you have not done so bad from your dad dying. You would have inherited all his cash," said Eli.

"This is through hard work and personal success," said Walter.

Walter now eyeball to eyeball with Eli. Until Eli spat in the face of Walter. With all his force Walter punched Eli in the stomach, wincing in pain, Eli stood back up.

"You are just like your father; he was also an evil and horrible individual. I hope he rots in hell just like you," laughed Eli.

Chapter 27

Another gunshot could be heard just as Dan arrived in Walter's office. Looking out of the floor to ceiling window, seeing the workers oblivious to the mayhem of what was going on here. One of the workers waved to Dan without a clue what was going on just behind these walls.

"Hello," a small echoey voice could be heard. Dan with a shocked face wondering where it was coming from.

"Hello, can you hear me."

"Can you hear me," the voice could be heard again.

Dan headed over to the wall with the newspaper cut outs. Suddenly he could feel a draught coming from the wall behind a mirror.

Dan always noticed this mirror. It was used by Walter to proudly look at himself and admire the success that he created. Usually had a glass of drink in his hand and a cigar in his mouth.

However, there was something unusual about the mirror now with a sense of cold air coming from it.

"Hello, is anyone there," the voice could be heard again.

Dan rushed to put his ear against the mirror.

Standing back, he took the mirror off the wall.

Dan's face dropped with shock at what he was seeing in front of him. A rusty old door which as expected was locked.

He knew the voice was coming from behind the door. Wondering who the sick freak locked up behind the door.

Heading over to Walter's desk and raiding all the drawers to find a key for the door. Hopefully Walter was stupid enough to leave them lying around somewhere.

"Bingo," Dan said in a surprising way. Realising Walter was stupid after all to leave the keys lying around in an unlocked drawer in his office for all to see.

Heading back to the rusty old door, shaking in preparation of what they will expect to see.

It was quite a tricky lock to get open, but it started creaking and slowly opened to a dark, cold stairwell

Dan could hear whispering and rattling as he headed down the stairs.

The strangest setup was awaiting him at the bottom of the stairs. It looked like somebody was living in Squalor.

A table for two with a wilted flower in a vase as the centrepiece with some dirty plates left there.

"Hello, I need some help," the voice could be heard again

Turning around, Dan could hear banging on a closed door behind him. Trying to open the door without success.

"Hold on, I will try to unlock it," shouted Dan.

Quickly getting the keys out of his pocket, shaking trying to locate the correct one.

"I think I have it," Dan said whilst turning the lock on the door.

The door opened and stood in front of him was a blonde woman who looked unwashed, with grubby straggly hair.

"Are you okay," a concerned Dan asked the woman. Looking round the room, a double bed which was unmade with a bathroom. Clothes everywhere, it did look like a person had been squatting here without a care in the world. However, this woman was clearly in distress.

"Yes, I am fine. At last, a different person I have seen in years," the woman said.

"Who are you," Dan asked the woman.

With panic in her voice, the woman gulped and looked up at Dan.

"My name is Kathryn."

Dan gasped with utter shock and disbelief on his face.

"You mean Kathryn, the former fiancé of Walter," asked Dan.

"Yes. That is me," replied Kathryn.

Chapter 28

Both are still in shock, sitting at the end of the bed. Dan now comforted Kathryn with an arm and a blanket around her shoulders.

"What has he done to you? How long have you been here for," asked Dan.

"About ten years. Stuck down here the only person I have had contact with, is Walter," said Kathryn.

"How did you end up down here," said Dan, now looking more confused.

"Not necessarily just stuck down here. I have been in his office a few times. It basically started about ten years ago. Out of the blue Walter contacted me. I had not heard from him since we went our separate ways," Kathryn was explaining.

"Was that quite soon after the night you got raped. Walter told me this. I am sorry," Dan looked very apologetic whilst feeling sorry for Kathryn.

"Yes. Neither of us coped with the aftermath of that night. We went our separate ways.

Like I said he contacted me and invited me to his island to reconcile. He was always impulsive when it came to wooing me," smiled Kathryn.

Dan did remember a story of his first date with Kathryn when he flew her by helicopter to a restaurant in New York.

I arrived on the island and after a couple of nights together he went a bit strange and obsessive.

He drugged me and I woke up down here, in this makeshift flat.

"Did he ever, you know. Without your consent," asked Dan.

"No. God no. Not that I am aware anyway. At first it was very much consented. He would come down here and we would have a meal together on the table out there. After that I would fall asleep quite early most nights and wake up with door locked. Kathryn now started to look a bit upset.

Dan knew that this was the devious behaviour of a man who has become obsessed and kidnapped a victim and manipulating them to do what they want.

"Kathryn, you need help. It is not right what he has done. Honestly, it's quite psychopathic and obsessive," said Dan who was now getting even more concerned for Kathryn. Looking at the cuts and bruises on her wrists.

"The police are on their way now and hopefully this ordeal will be over," explained Dan.

He helped her up and started to escort her up the cellar steps.

At the top they faced a gun.

"What the hell is going on," yelled Walter. Aiming a gun towards his potential next victim.

Chapter 29

"You traitor," shouted Walter as Dan and Kathryn scurried into the office.

"Everything I have done for you. This is how you repay me." Walter now getting angrier towards Dan.

"Walter, you are unwell. You have killed your guests and kidnapped the love of your life. It's over. The police are on their way now, you must hand yourself in," stated Dan. Who now was holding up a disoriented Kathryn.

"Look what you've done to her," said Dan more confidently, moving towards Walter.

At that moment helicopters could be seen landing on the island and a stampede of police could be heard heading through the corridor towards the office.

Walter standing there looking confused.

"All I wanted was to get justice for the misfortunes in my life," Walter now looking a bit more concerned of his actions.

"You have got justice but now these people must get justice over you," said Dan who gradually removed the gun from Walter.

The police barged through the door.

"Walter Newman you are under arrest for murder," shouted the officer.

Dan and Kathryn were whisked away. Walter stood there with handcuffs on, watching his empire collapse around him. Taking one final look at the newspaper cut outs on the wall. Walter turned to Dan and smiled.

Chapter 30

"We pulled up a cage out of the water with a dead person. There was also a burnt corpse in a room, one in the cellar with knife wounds all over the body. Must be from the walls in there as the psycho placed knives over both sets of walls. Looks like the walls crushed him." The inspector advised.

" Is that all Sir," the other officer asked.

"Further inspection there were two other people who are dead, looks like they have both been shot. "

" Sir, does that mean we have five in total?" the officer said.

" At the moment, yes. The investigation team are doing some further checks across the island. Using this and the testimony that Dan as provided I think that could be it," said the inspector.

"What about the woman," asked the officer.

"She was locked in a dungeon for years. She has gone for specialist help. Let her get that first and then we will question her on what she knows."

The inspector turned to the smashed window looking down on the island, watching forensics move bodies. Total chaos it was.

Turning back to the officer and whispering with satisfaction.

" Walter Newman who would have thought it."

Chapter 31

"Using the recommendation of the jury and laws of the state for this type of crime. My recommendation is that you should not see till the end of your life."

The judge clearly explaining the sentence, to a smiling Walter, sitting in the dock throughout the entire proceedings.

"The crimes you committed are despicable. Part of a sick game, making innocent people part of this. To top it off you put your ex-fiancé in a horrible situation, leaving her locked up in a dungeon. Giving her years of abuse for your own satisfaction. All part of a perverse game."

The judge at this point was seething, relaying back the actions to a disgusted courtroom.

"For the killing of five people and the kidnap and imprisonment of Kathryn Sinclair. I sentence you to death."

The Judge shouted as the gavel slammed on the table.

The courtroom cheered. Walter Newman smirked at the judge.

"You will remain in prison till the date of execution which will be decided at a later date."

With a vengeful look on his face, the judge looked at a Walter and muttered.

"Justice has been served,"

Printed in Great Britain
by Amazon